splinter

Copyright © 2017 by MICHAEL BUSSA

All rights reserved. No part of this publication may be reproduced, distributed, or transmitted in any form or by any means, including photocopying, recording, or other electronic or mechanical methods, without the prior written permission of the publisher, except in the case of brief quotations embodied in critical reviews and certain other noncommercial uses permitted by copyright law.

Read*Write* Literary, LLC New York, NY

Acknowledgments

I offer special thanks to Celia Rhodes and Gerri Hammond for their good sportsmanship and contributions.

I called upon each one and asked them to give me a word, something that isn't heard every day, or maybe just a favorite word. In exchange, I offered to write them into the story as characters and explained that their character could be mundane, or sinister, I wouldn't disclose either way, but I promised that both characters would be important to the story. Celia gave me the word, "Duplicitous," and Gerri offered, "Petrified." Keep an eye out for their contributions. Both, Gerri, and Celia were good sports – thank you!

As always, my thanks to Nick, a loyal, supportive friend and brother in Christ.

"Show me a man who is sane and I will cure him for you – "

– Carl Gustav Jung

splinte*r*

By
Michael Bussa

June 1909

     The green corridor leading to Bader's office felt hollow and cavernous. Though the expansive facility had opened only months earlier, the walls already echoed cries for help that were yet to be. Even so, by darkness or daylight, one needed only to walk the halls, once, to feel the chilling cold of abandonment. The only real noises heard were those brought about by the clicking heels of busy nurses and their soft reverend whispers when they spoke to other staff members – or the "insane." It was "Institutionally unpleasant," as one nurse described it. "There aren't any pictures on the walls! There's nothing to look at around here but all these sick patients. How can we expect anyone to feel better in such dismal surroundings?"

#

"Do you know who I am?" Bader questioned while putting on his spectacles to review the chart before him. He waited patiently for a few moments but there was no response. He scribbled on his clipboard and sipped from his steaming coffee cup, then carefully placed it on a coaster. He was both, frustrated and fascinated with the case. He smiled and tried again.

"I'm Dr. Bader, do you remember me from yesterday?"

The boy sat quietly in his wheelchair. He watched the tree branch outside the window as it swayed back and forth in the wind, clawing at the glass. Bader pulled his chair closer.

"I know that you've been through something difficult; something that I want to understand if you'll help me. Will you help me?" He paused. "Do you remember what happened at home that night – what happened to your sister and father, I mean?"

The boy remained still, without expression as he had during each session for over three months. His only progress was moving from a catatonic state to his present condition. Not much better, in fact. Adam was detached, not irreparable, however. The diagnosis was psychogenic amnesia, with periodic blackouts, some lasting for days. When it appeared that the amnesia was gone, except for a few lapses, the blackouts increased – sometimes dramatically, but Bader was committed and determined. He was empirical by training and, it seemed, by his very nature, in that he did not take a philosophical approach to the treatment of the insane. Adam's case was what he trained for and he was ready to dig deep into it. But the boy was fragile. It was too soon after the incident so, Bader adjusted his level of patience, remembering that Adam was, after all, still a boy.

Bader let out a long sigh, then put his hand on the boy's shoulder, offering a comforting squeeze. "It's all right. No one can hurt you while you're here. I'll call for your nurse; she'll take you back to your room. I care for you, Adam. I care very much. We'll try again tomorrow."

Bader pressed a button next to the telephone and moments later the nurse appeared and wheeled Adam out of the room. It was Adam's seventh birthday, though it would have been inappropriate to celebrate.

Bader opened the top drawer of his desk and pulled out a folder labeled 'Adam X.' He opened it and saw the police report. Although he had reviewed it ad nauseam, he took another look, shaking his head as he thumbed through it. *Unbelievable.*

"I've got to get a hold of the original police report," he whispered to himself. An even bigger obstacle since Adam was a minor.

#

July 1930

Adam looked into the mirror as he ran a brush through his hair, then pulled the lint from his pants. He wheeled over to the closet and reached down to the floor for his shoes. He placed them in his lap and rolled into the parlor to wait. Miss Gerri was always kind enough to put his shoes on for him. He looked forward to Wednesdays; it was Bingo night. There wasn't much else for a paraplegic to do in the small town of Milnor, North Dakota.

"Oh, no – she's late. She's late, again. Oh, no, not today – please!" But she had never once been late. Adam had a quirk. He waited every week for Gerri to drive over from the church to pick him up. And every week he would go through the same routine. He grabbed the wheels and rocked back and forth, then looked up at the clock, then out the window and he would go through the routine until she arrived.

"Oh! C'mon, Miss Gerri, please don't – "

" – Shut up!" a voice shrieked from behind. "Just stop

it, you whiny little ingrate! You're lucky she takes you! *I* certainly wouldn't. Now hush up!"

" – What are you doing here, Ada? I begged you to stay away for a while."

" – That's no way to welcome someone who's put her life on hold to cater to your every need. Besides, my room is upstairs. Would you have me sleep in the tool shed?"

" – Would you? Please? I must say, Ada, there's nothing like a meddlesome, uncaring sister to brighten one's life. New hair color, I see. Blonde makes you look like a tired old flapper."

She walked over to him, reached for his collar and tugged gently at each side. "Perfect," she said, with a toothy smile. She combed her fingers through his hair when he pushed her away.

" – Stop touching me!"

She put her hand over her heart and feigned a humbling face.

" Am I so uncaring that I can't bear to sit around watching you pick through your plastic chips, chattering with the old hags about their ailments and their meatloaf recipes? Yes, as a matter-of-fact, I am so uncaring. G49; G54; Gee, I'm bored! You can have it."

" – Good, then leave. I'm not strong enough to deal with you today, Ada. Just go. Miss Gerri interrupts her schedule to get me to the church twice a week and she does it faithfully and without complaining. So, you see, I don't need you. Never did."

Ada began singing. Adam hated it and that's why she did it. It was always the same tune, "Ba ba black sheep have you any wool – "

Adam felt the stir of anger as Ada mocked him with laughter.

" – STOP IT!" he screamed. You know she used to sing that song to me before bed. Is that why you do it? You were always jealous of me!"

" – Oh, baby brother – still in denial. You know there never was a 'she' to sing to you. It was always daddy. He used to –"

" – SHUT UP, ADA! I told you not to talk about him! Never! You promised," he reminded her.

Just then, the doorbell rang, and a slender woman with a full smile stepped inside.

" Hey, what's all the shouting about?" she quizzed.

" – Ada and I are having a disagreement."

She looked at Adam momentarily, then raised a brow. " –Again?" She appeared puzzled as they both looked around the room, but Ada was gone. *Good riddance.*

" Well, then, let's put the demon to bed and get to church, hmm?" She gave a hearty laugh.

"All set Adam?"

Adam nodded.

" Let's get your shoes on."

As she wheeled him toward the door, he saw Ada peeking out from behind it. She had her hand over her mouth, snickering. He clenched his teeth and held up his fist as they wheeled passed her.

#

"Adam!" Dr. Vann called out from across the table. His office was simple with minimal furnishings; a couch; a chair; a coffee table; and his desk. A few mismatched pictures and some Ivy League certificates hung in black frames against the putrid, green walls.

Adam was distracted. "Why do I hate green so much?

Do you know why I hate green so much, Doc?"

" – Adam, please focus. You need to try harder, today."

" – I'm afraid I'm not gonna be very much help. I feel... 'foggy'"

" – Try."

" – Dr. Vann, I'm telling you – "

" – We've still got 45 minutes on the clock, Adam, I'm not going to let you waste them. Focus on me, Adam. Look at me. Any blackouts that you know of? Any periods of time that you can't account for?"

Adam looked up at the ceiling. He pointed to each tile as he counted them aloud.

" ADAM!"

He turned his attention toward Vann, "Sorry, Doc." He waved his hand, motioning for Vann to continue.

" Let's work on what you can remember. We're just starting to make progress, Adam; these last three weeks have been excellent. I'll start you off. Last week, you told me that you remembered that your father staggered through the door that night. He stood in the parlor staring at Ada, staring into her eyes when he smacked the side of her head and she screamed. 'He was angry,' you said. 'Furious.' You told me that you remembered how he made his way to the kitchen and came back with the flat iron. Do you still remember it that way?"

Tears welled and Adam felt the debilitating fear of that night, returning.

" Look, Doc, I – "

" – Damn it, Adam! I want to help you. Do you want to go through the rest of your life feeling the way you do? Now, let's continue."

Adam gestured with a finger that he needed a moment. He felt a lump in his throat. He took a sip of water and sighed. "I do, I still remember it the way you said it. Yes, just that way."

Adam grabbed the wheels and rolled over to the window. He closed his eyes and put his hand on the glass. It felt cold and soothing against his palm.

"Doc... I think there's something else that's coming back to me, now. Yes. I can see his dirty face right now, as it was that night. But... now I remember that as he started for the kitchen, he turned to look at me – I was peeking around the corner. His face changed, you know? It looked... monstrous. He came over to me. He smelled bad. I remember that I was so scared I wet my pajamas. I was cornered so I couldn't run. He bent down and whispered."

Tears streamed down Adam's face as he sobbed.

" Go on, Adam. Don't stop."

Adam took a deep breath, let it out slowly and continued, " As I said, he bent down and whispered something awful. His eyes were like an animal's eyes. I can see them. I can still see them right now. He looked right into my eyes and said, 'get ready, you're next.'" Adam wiped the tears as they rolled down his face and he sobbed. Vann quickly went to him. He put his hand on Adams' shoulder. "Good, Adam. You did very well, today. Remember, he's long gone and there's no way he can harm you now. You accomplished a lot, today, Adam, I'm proud of you."

Vann called for the nurse to bring some water and aspirins. He continued to praise Adam for working so hard. It was a significant breakthrough. But there was much more to Adam's memory than he shared that day.

The door latched closed as Adam left the office. Vann picked up the telephone.

"Nurse, I need to get in touch with a Dr. Bader. He's registered with the State Sanitarium in Dunseith, up in the

Turtle Mountains. Call me back when you reach him."

#

It was 3:03 when Adam looked at the clock on the nightstand. Like so many other nights, he had difficulty sleeping. He rubbed his eyes to focus. The streetlight offered just enough light to assist. The quiet was maddening, to Adam. He couldn't stand darkness, or quiet. He knew that it would only take one press of the button next to the clock and Ada would come stomping down the stairs to admonish him. She would announce that if it weren't an emergency, she would make his life a living hell. She was pure vinegar, that one. Even so, her company was better than the darkness and quiet. He hated to depend on her but, she was all he had. As much as their relationship had soured since that horrific night twenty-one years earlier, it was that very night that bound them with a common ground. Adam didn't know whether he could survive without her.

He pressed the button and a few moments of silence passed. He pressed it twice more and there it was, the pounding footsteps and the creaking of the wooden staircase.

The bedroom door swung open, and she appeared with her hand covering a yawn.

"What?!" she demanded.

" – I can't sleep. I thought you might put on some tea."

" – You know, Adam, this act of yours is getting old. You can get yourself into – and out of – that chair. Everybody knows it. So you can certainly warm the water yourself!"

" – Okay. It's all right; I'll manage. I'm not feeling strong enough, that's all."

" – What is it, Adam?" Ada seemed genuinely concerned. "I'm sorry. If you need me to, I'll put some water on. Stay there and I'll be back to get you."

As Ada disappeared through the door, Adam pushed himself into an upright position, then used both arms to transfer himself into the wheelchair. He stretched and yawned as he noticed the half moon outside the window.

The pot whistled as Adam wheeled into the kitchen. "Ada?" There was no response. He rolled over to the stove to turn the flame off. He called for her twice, still, no reply. There was no urgency since It wasn't out of character for her to turn from warm to cold; It was her way, as he came to accept it. He poured the hot water and steeped the tea bag for a few minutes. His eyes panned the kitchen and he yawned as he came into focus. He listened for the slightest stirring. The silence had returned. *She must have gone back to bed,* he surmised. He noticed that the cutlery drawer was open and rolled over to close it when he saw that the butcher knife was gone.

#

Vann's morning started as soon as he hung his jacket and hat. The head nurse called and he picked up on the first ring.

"Yes?"

" – Dr. Vann, I was able to reach Dr. Bader's office. Unfortunately, he's away on temporary leave. His secretary said that if it was urgent, you could contact him at the Valley City State University. He'll be lecturing there through the month. I can get them on the phone if you'd like."

" – Thank you, that won't be necessary." He hung up and thought for a moment as he glanced at his watch. He tapped a pen on the desk as he thought for a moment, then called the nurse back. "On second thought, I'll need you to clear my schedule for the rest of the day, and for tomorrow. I'm going to drive over to Valley City, tonight. Can you please make a reservation for me at the Hotel Rudolf? It's at the corner of Central and Second St."

" – Yes, Doctor, right away."

#

Adam felt his spirits lift as he rolled into the kitchen that morning. A brilliant sun beamed through sparkling glass. When he opened the window to let in some fresh air, he spotted his neighbor, Celia, waving to him from her garden. She had become his most trusted confidant.

Adam assumed that Ada was already up and about when he smelled ammonia and saw the mop and bucket that sat in the corner. The kitchen was spotless. Ada rarely ate breakfast so, Adam knew enough not to wait around for her. He started a pan of water on the stove for oatmeal, then rolled back to the table and picked up the newspaper. It was odd, she never brought it inside unless he complained first, but there it was.

"Ada?" he called out. No response. He wheeled to the

back door and pulled the curtain to look out into the yard. He called out, again, "ADA!" Still, nothing.

The doorbell rang and the door was pushed slightly ajar. "Adam?" It was Miss Gerri. Adam quickly rolled toward the parlor.

"Oh, Miss Gerri, Ada's disappeared again. Why does she do this to me? She mocks me and torments me, then vanishes without any explanation when she returns."

" – Well, Adam, I've always made it my business to remain neutral in such family matters, but I think a better question to ask is, 'why do you let her'?"

#

The small cafe was potent with the smell of freshly brewed coffee. The afternoon sun shined across the checkered tablecloth, and the clatter of dishes could be heard coming from the kitchen.

"Thank you for meeting with me Dr. Bader, I am sorry for the short notice but as I said when I called from the hotel, it is a matter of urgency." Vann motioned to the waitress.

"What is this concerning? I certainly didn't think you

drove all the way from Milnor to make small talk."

" – Right, well, I must apologize that I wasn't forthcoming on the phone. I'm here about one of my patients," Vann started, as he fished into his pocket for a small notepad. "It's an odd case, shrouded in mystery. My patient's name is Adam. His records arrived from your facility marked only, 'Adam X,' nothing else."

Bader became visibly agitated. He quickly stood up and pulled a dollar bill from his pocket, then threw it on the table.

"If you had told me this on the telephone I would have told you to get in your car and go back home."

" –Please, Dr. Bader, allow me a few moments of professional courtesy – please?" He motioned for Bader to sit.

Reluctantly, Bader took his seat, again. The waitress appeared with a coffee pot and two glasses of water and Bader slid his cup toward her. Vann ordered a salad and she hurried off to another table.

Bader sipped his coffee, nervously. He was clearly uncomfortable talking about Adam. He placed the cup on the saucer and tapped his fingers on the table as he looked about the cafe. Then he focused his attention directly on Vann.

"There is little I can tell you," he said.

" – Dr. Bader, I've been seeing Adam for six months. I don't know how to help him. I have nothing to work with – to reference. It has been strange from the start – my relationship with Adam, I mean. You'll probably think I'm away from my senses when I tell you that I'm paid for my services to Adam by– "

Bader interrupted. "You're paid, for your services to Adam, each week, in cash, and it comes to you in an envelope with no return address. Isn't that correct? I can see by the puzzled look on your face that it is. You may continue with your sessions, however, you do have the option to call the telephone number that comes each week in that same envelope and tell them that you want to drop his case – for your benefit, I would advise the latter."

Vann shook his head and looked down at the table, then back up at Bader. "You see, this is what I'm talking about. You're as secretive and evasive as everyone involved with Adam."

" – Dr. Vann, when I received the police report twenty-one years ago, all of the censored script that rendered the most crucial details of that night, unreadable, left me having to read between the lines – an impossible feat with Adam's case, as you must certainly know. I am aware that there was a criminal incident involving Adam, his father, and his sister, Ada. There was no information offered about his mother or any other relatives, and none came forward while he was under state care. It was the most confounded case that I have ever been involved in."

The waitress stepped up with her coffee pot and refilled Bader's cup.

"Anything else for you two?" She looked at each one and smiled.

" – No, thank you," Vann replied.

" – You two have a pleasant afternoon. C'mon back, soon." She smiled again. She placed the check on the table and removed Vann's half-eaten salad. As she stepped away, Vann noticed when she looked back at them from the corner of her eye in a most curious way.

Vann was about to speak when Bader held his hand up to stop him.

" – There's more," Bader said. "When I questioned the police and asked for more data the officer explained that all records attached to the case were sealed by court order, indefinitely. Additionally, there was a gag order on all of the policemen involved, leaving the press unable to obtain, or report, any details of the crime. Have you ever heard such nonsense?"

" – But what can – "

" – I have only one final offering. Adam can be endearing, but make no mistake, there is an underlying element that lines his personality. It is something that seems out of his control and it poses a threat to those around him. I've seen it. Now, I have nothing more. Please don't contact me again, though they probably already know that you did."

" – Who are *they*?" questioned Vann.

Bader tossed his napkin on the table and started for the door when suddenly he stopped for a moment, and returned. He looked around the cafe nervously, then looked back at Vann. "Dr. Vann, have you... met Ada?"

" – No, though I have asked for her to come to some of the sessions she refused. Adam says that she finds me to be a threat and interference with their family."

" – Take her for her word."

" – You've met her then?" Vann asked as he stood to put on his jacket.

" – Good day, Dr. Vann." Bader hurried out the door.

#

Vann paid the check, then walked next door to the hotel. There was a strident warning in Bader's message and Vann's curiosity was piqued. Bader didn't offer much. He seemed to be holding back. And after their conversation, Vann had more clarity on his own suspicion. He thought that all of the mystery surrounding Adam might be narrowed down to one of two possibilities: That somebody, somewhere, was getting paid – but why? The other possibility was that someone in the family would have been embarrassed by a criminal incident, possibly someone known to the public. *Who was Adam's father?* He wondered.

As he walked across the hotel lobby, he heard a young woman call from the front desk,
"Excuse me, sir, are you Dr. Vann?"

He turned to face her, " – Yes, I am."

" – Doctor, there was a call about twenty minutes ago, a young woman, I think. She asked if you were staying here. I told her I would take a message when she hung up, abruptly. I'm sorry, she didn't give her name."

Back at the cafe, the waitress returned to the table and

picked up Vann's notebook he had left behind. She made her way to the back of the cafe, then placed the notebook in front of a lone figure and continued toward the kitchen.

#

Gerri stepped into the parlor where Adam sat ready with a small box of bingo chips. She was shaking.

"Adam," she blotted the tears from her eyes. "I'm not going to be able to take you to Bingo today; it's been canceled. I know it's disappointing to you and I'm sorry."

" – Canceled? Why, is there something wrong?" Adam had trouble handling changes in his routine. He immediately felt the edging of anxiety.

" – Adam, something has happened – something terrible. You know Mr. Douglas from Bingo?"

" – Who doesn't? You can't be as mean as he is and go unnoticed. Once, when Ada walked past his house in her new dress, he told her it was too short, then he called her a little trollop who wasn't fit to live in his town. Can you believe it? His town."

" – Adam, listen to me for a moment. I have difficult

news to deliver. Mr. Douglas was murdered last night in his bed. It's all over town. It was in this morning's newspaper." She continued to sob as she dabbed her eyes with a tissue.

" – Murdered?" Adam looked over her shoulder, and up past the top of the stairs at Ada's bedroom door. He looked back at Miss Gerri. "Well, you know," he started with a nervous tremble in his voice. "He wasn't just a mean-spirited old man, the word around town is that he was involved in something shady, something about loans. Someone like him is bound to have enemies, don't you think? Can I make you some tea? Since we can't go to Bingo, I'd like it if you'd stay for while."

Tea? she thought. Gerri was surprised by Adam's reaction to the news. It was a horrible tragedy, no matter what kind of person he was. A tragedy for anyone to have their life taken in that way.

" –No, no, I'm sorry, Adam. I can't stay. This is very upsetting to me, I've got to get home. The thought of what happened to him in that bedroom leaves me petrified. I can't imagine – No, I just can't imagine. Will you be alright, Adam?"

" – It's all right, you go on home. I'll be fine, thank you for coming over, Miss Gerri."

She stepped outside and Adam closed the door behind her. He exhaled in relief. He didn't think he could keep up appearances much longer. The news stirred kindred emotions that he didn't want to deal with. He took a deep breath and let it out. A wave of fear moved through him leaving him dizzy. He closed his eyes as he thought about the events of the past couple of days. He felt the bile rise as an icy chill traveled down his spine. He was afraid of what he was thinking. He rolled back into the kitchen to read the details in the newspaper:

> *Joseph Douglas was found dead in his home on 5th Avenue near Main, at around 4:00 am, with multiple stab wounds to the face and chest. Sargent County Police say "This is a brutal murder, something we don't see in our community...*

Adam couldn't bear to read another word. His senses were reeling and he quickly looked over at the cutlery drawer. He felt a cold sweat on his forehead as he rolled over and grabbed the handle, took a deep breath, then let it out slowly.

He quickly drew it open and his eyes widened in horror as his stomach sank. The butcher knife was back in its place.

"ADAAAAA!! WHAT HAVE YOU DONE?!!

#

The door opened and the nurse padded across Vann's office. Just as she placed a message on the desk, a hand came to rest on her shoulder.

"Oh, Dr. Vann," she held her hand over her heart. "You gave me quite a start. I was leaving you this message. I just received an urgent call from Dr. Bader. He said that he had thought about the situation very seriously. He stated that he has a packet of information that you should see, and that it should be as soon as possible. He said that you should not call, that he was driving over to deliver it personally. He called about ten minutes ago from the road."

"Alright, thank you," he replied. The nurse returned to her station. Vann felt his heart race with anxiety. Hand-delivered information in his field of work was often grave. Just then, the phone rang.

"Yes, Nurse."

" – Dr. Vann, Adam just called and I'm afraid he's canceled his appointment for today. Shall I get him back on the phone?"

" – Yes... wait, no, on second thought, I'm going to take a ride over to see him. Thank you."

"Doctor, one more thing. He sounded... different."

" – Different? How so?"

" – Well, I don't mean anything by it, but he sounded effeminate. I'm not certain it was him, and I'm not certain it wasn't. And another thing – just before he hung up I would swear that I heard him singing."

" – Singing? What was he singing?"

" – It sounded like, 'Ba ba black sheep.'"

Vann hung up and grabbed his jacket as he hurried out the door.

#

Adam was frantically rocking back and forth in his chair. His face was wet with tears and he shook uncontrollably when Ada appeared in the room. "Ada... Ada, what are we going to do? I know what you did! I know! This is why I told you to stay away. Why don't you listen to me? You never listen to me!"

" – SHUT UP, ADAM! Or I'll make sure you can't talk! And you won't be seeing Dr. Vann anymore, I'll see to that, too. He's prying – asking way too many questions! He's trying to make you think that *you're* crazy. How laughable that is when everyone knows that I'm the crazy one."

" – He means well, Ada, He's a good doctor. Leave him alone! I get scared when you act like this. Go, Ada! Go away for awhile! Please, I'm begging you to leave him alone! I like him; he helps me."

" – He helps me," she mocked, in a childish voice. Ada slapped him as her face grew red.

Adam was shocked as he quickly put his hand to his cheek to soothe the sting. He grabbed the wheels to back away from her when she blocked him with her foot. She snarled and slapped him harder. Adam wrapped both arms around his head to protect himself. She was out of control. She pointed her finger at his face. "You're going up to my room, brother! And you know what? You're never coming down!" She rushed him toward the staircase.

The murder stirred more activity than the Sargent County Police had seen in months. A police officer knocked twice, then entered the office and dropped a report on the desk, along with a large, thick envelope.

" – Oswalt, I checked the registration for the plate on the car that went off the road outside of town on Highway 13. It belongs to a Dr. William Bader, of Dunseith. Identification on his person confirms the same. He died on impact. The body is on its way to Dakota Clinic in Fargo. The only thing in the car was this envelope with the word 'Vann' written on it. Boy, that was some accident. He had to be doing over a hundred when he lost control."

Oswalt looked up. " – Assuming, he lost control. Vann? Isn't that the name of the psychiatrist at the clinic in Milnor? I'll give 'em a call and see if he knows anything about it."

#

Vann pulled up to the large white house. As he headed

for the front door, he briefly saw the curtains move in the window on the second floor. He caught a glimpse of Ada's blonde hair as she quickly turned away and drew the curtain closed. He rang the bell and waited for a moment. He rang a second time and waited. There was no response. He called out, "Adam!" He rang once more, then knocked repeatedly. "ADAM! IT'S DR. VANN! I NEED TO TALK TO YOU, ADAM!...ADAM!!

Just then, he heard the upstairs window slide open. He stepped back and looked up to the second floor when he saw Ada throw a flat iron aimed directly at him. He jumped out of the way just before it hit him. "ADA! What's the matter with you!? Where's Adam? ADA!"

The window slammed closed and the curtains were drawn, once more. Vann got back in his car and returned to the clinic, stopping at the nurse's station before heading to his office.

"Nurse, can you please get the police on the phone?"

" – I can save you the time, Doctor, they're waiting in your office."

Dr. Vann? I'm officer Oswalt from the Sargent County Police." He extended his hand to Vann. "Doctor, there's been an accident outside of town involving a Dr. William Bader. Did you know him?"

" – Did?" Vann felt a knot in his stomach.

" – Unfortunately, he didn't survive the crash. From the wreckage, it appeared that he was traveling at a pretty good clip."

" – Well, I am genuinely saddened to hear the news, he was a very respected man in his field. What a shock this is." Vann felt as though he had taken a punch to the gut. "I am sorry. Please tell me what it is that I can do for you, Officer?"

" – Doctor, It seems odd that a medical doctor, who knows, first hand, the consequences of reckless driving, would be traveling along the highway at such a dangerously high speed. It seems equally odd, almost mysterious, that under that circumstance, he carried nothing with him in the entire car, except this package marked 'Vann,' wouldn't you agree?"

" – Yes, well, as a matter of fact, Officer, he was bringing the package to me. I'm terribly saddened by the news of his death. He and I were working together on a case, and this is crucial information that will help me. You see, I'm a psychiatrist, and this information pertains to one of my patients. So, do I need to sign something to take possession of it?

" – I'm afraid it won't be quite so simple, Dr. Vann. I'll need to hang on to it until I complete my report. It shouldn't be more than a couple of days. In the meantime, I appreciate your verifying the information for me, you've been helpful."

The officer shook his hand and left Vann's office. He paused momentarily outside the door, then left the building.

Vann was rattled over the news of Bader, and he knew there was something critical in the package that Bader wanted him to see immediately. If Bader's death was no accident, he wondered, then, if it was possible that *his* life was in danger, too? "What was it that Bader said in the cafe about our meeting?" he mumbled to himself. *'They probably already know that you've contacted me.'*

Vann slapped his hand to his forehead. He was so disturbed by the visit, he forgot about Adam. He quickly headed for the door, hoping to catch Officer Oswalt when the telephone rang.

"Dr. Vann?" Adam's tone was unusually solemn, and

controlled.

" – Oh, Adam, I'm so glad you called. I'd like to – "

" – Dr. Vann, I just want to apologize for Ada. I know you came by today when I was resting and Ada told me that she wasn't very kind to you. She wants you to know that she's sorry. She's had a terrible time of it, lately, Dr. Vann – a terrible time, but she is sorry." Just then, Adam began whispering, "Dr. Vann, can you hear me?"

" – Yes Adam, but – "

He became frantic, " – Oh my God, Dr. Vann, please, help me! It's Ada. She's gone to the dark place, again. Dr. Vann she's trying to kill me, I'm sure of – " The line went dead.

Vann slammed the phone to the receiver and bolted out of the office. As he ran down the hall past the nurse's station they looked at each other, puzzled. The head nurse hurried out from behind the counter, then rushed to the corridor.

"DR. VANN!!" He continued running. She threw her arm up in the air and turned to the other nurse, "Good heavens, what is going on around here?"

#

Vann's car screeched to a halt in Adam's driveway and he jumped out of the car, when he heard a voice calling out from next door,

"Hello...over here!" Celia called.

Vann hurried across the grass to the front porch where she was sitting in a wicker chair.

"I'm Celia... Celia Rose." She extended her hand, as a lady would. "I just wanted to save you the trouble. You see, they're gone. You must be Dr. Vann?"

" – Gone? Do you know where they went?" Vann asked, scratching his eyebrow.

" – Oh, they'll be back, shortly, they've gone marketing. Can I offer you some raspberry lemonade, in the meantime? I make it freshly squeezed – no bitter pulp." she snickered.

" – Well, you say they'll be back shortly, huh? Sure, why not? Yes, I am Dr. Vann."

She opened the screen door and Vann followed close behind. Once inside, the sharp scent of ammonia stung his nostrils.

" – Forgive the smell, gotta keep a clean house, you understand. Let's go out to the garden, I think that'll be nicer."

Celia led him down a dark hall, filled with dozens of pictures from her garden. She motioned with her hand for him to go first, and when he stepped outside he was taken by surprise. It was a glorious, English garden with a winding path all the way back to the tool shed. She walked him halfway through when they came to a bench. She motioned for him to sit.

" – Now, isn't this nicer than waiting in a car?"

" – Very nice, yes, it is. You must spend all of your time tending to these beautiful flowers."

She was glowing with pride when she turned to him. "You know, the real secret is: good fertilizer. Yes, good fertilizer will send your garden reaching for the sky."

Just then her two curious cats came to rub against his leg. One jumped up on the bench next to him, purring. He began nudging Vann's arm with his nose.

" – Now don't mind them, next to Adam, these are my very best friends, Duck, and Goose. I'll be back in a moment, now don't you stray." She hurried off toward the house.

Vann felt confused and concerned. On the telephone, Adam was frantic and sounded to be in impendent danger. The two of them going off to the market doesn't fit that scenario.

What was going on?

Celia returned and placed a tray on the table next to Vann. There were two drinks and a plate of cookies. Vann took a couple of quick gulps, then replaced the glass on the tray.

"That does hit the spot. Hot day, today."

" – Warmer is better, as you can see by my measure – the garden, I mean," she smiled.

"Do you live here alone, Celia?"

" – Just the three of us," she chuckled.

" – What do you do with your day when you're not gardening?"

" – Oh, I enjoy photography and I dabble in paint. Idle hands... and all that."

Vann smiled, " I understand. Surely you must feel lonely at times?"

" – No, not unusually so. You see, that's why I'm so grateful to have Adam right next door. He is the dearest boy. Then there's Ada, she's a handful for most, not for me–"

" – Miss Rose, I'm gravely concerned. You see, I received a distressing call earlier from Adam. He gave me the impression that he was in trouble."

" – Trouble? Really? Well, did he tell you anything else?" she tilted her head paying close attention. Vann thought she seemed almost amused.

" – Miss Rose, I – "

" – Oh, I haven't been Miss Rose in a lifetime, call me Celia – please."

" – Celia, how well would you say you know Adam and Ada?"

She lit up a smile, " Why, I can tell you with all certainty that no one knows them as I do. No one! I know every intimate detail of their tragic lives."

Tragic? He thought. She must know them well to use such a description.

" – Celia, I have a great conflict here. On the one hand, I'm sworn to keep the confidentiality of a patient. On the other hand, I genuinely care very deeply for Adam and if you know him as you do, then I believe you could be instrumental in helping me to help him. But we're back to the confidentiality of records. I feel quite torn." He finished his drink and placed it back on the tray, then took a handkerchief out of his pocket and blotted his forehead.

"You haven't touched your almond cookies." She lifted

the tray and held it closer.

" – Oh, thank you for offering, I don't think so. But if it isn't too much trouble, I wouldn't mind another glass of that lemonade."

" – It's no trouble, I'll be right back." She picked up the tray and disappeared up the garden path.

#

Oswalt was busy with the accident report when his attention focused on Vann's envelope. He cut open the package hoping that there may be some clues to indicate that there was more to Bader's death than accidental. He read, paying close attention to details. Adam's father was killed by blunt force. The weapon was believed to be a flat iron. When Adam was a year old, his mother was taken to a state mental facility when she went mad after her doctor diagnosed her with tuberculosis. Later she improved and her doctors agreed there was an apparent misdiagnosis.

Her psychiatrist, Dr. Bader, called her "cunning," and "elusive." He did not feel that she had made a full mental recovery. Months later, she went missing and after several years, was believed to be dead. Adam lived alone with his father until that night when he was taken into state care. He remained in the Dunseith facility until his eighteenth birthday. An assessment determined at that time that he did not pose a threat to society, or himself, and he was released.

Oswalt decided to get the envelope to Vann immediately. There didn't appear to be any details that would indicate foul play in the death of Bader. He felt no need to keep the information away from Vann any longer than necessary. He headed back to Vann's office.

#

Celia set the tray on the counter and opened the cabinet, then pushed a few items out of the way. She reached to the back and pulled out a small box, then opened it and sprinkled some granules into Vann's drink. She quickly stirred it when she looked out the window into the garden, "Such a beautiful day," she proclaimed. She threw a few chips of ice in the glass, then picked up the tray. She turned around and backed out the screen door, taking care not to spill. She headed back down the garden path to Vann.

"Here we are, Dr. Vann. Sip it slowly – last two glasses."

" – I think Adam is lucky to have you, Celia. I'm sure you're there whenever he needs anything."

" – Oh, to the contrary. I'm the lucky one, Doctor. Why just the other day I needed him to run an errand for me and do you know that he ran right over – didn't waste a moment."

Vann wasn't sure he heard her. " – You said 'he ran'?"

" – Well, most of the time he walks, but I told him to hurry so, he ran."

#

Oswalt carried the package inside the clinic to the nurses station.

"Yes, Officer?"

"Nurse, I'm Oswalt, I called for Dr. Vann earlier."

"Oh, yes. I'm sorry but he hasn't returned yet. You can leave the package on his desk if you'd like. I'll take you down there."

" – No, that's all right, Nurse, it's important that I give it to him personally."

" – I understand. If you'd like you can have a seat over there." She pointed to a waiting area. "I'd be more than happy to fetch some coffee, how do you take it?"

" – No, don't trouble yourself, I'm fine."

" – You know," she began, with a chuckle. "You should have been here earlier when he left, you could have arrested him for speeding down the hall," she giggled.

" – What do you mean?"

" – Well, right after he received a call from his patient, Adam, he took off like a bat outta hell – never said a word as he passed me in a blur."

Oswalt jumped up from his seat and ran down the corridor, then burst through the exit door.

She turned to the other nurse. "You know this place really is a madhouse!"

#

" Celia, are you telling me he gets out of his chair?" Vann was stunned.

" – Adam has walked ever since I've known him. You

see, that chair keeps them from coming for him."

" – Keeps who from – "

Her demeanor changed, abruptly. She became controlled and deliberate. Her voice took a sinister tone when she stood up. Vann felt weak and dizzy. He was losing focus when the garden became a blur of colors in motion. He grabbed the armrest for balance.

" What's happening, here. Suddenly, I'm not feeling well, Celia. Can you call – "

" – I knew that there was something about you, Vann. I couldn't quite place a finger on it at first, but once you involved Bader, I knew you were one of them."

" – Please, I don't know what you're talking about," he struggled, as he was overcome by fear and nausea.

" – I suspected you were going to be trouble from the moment you started seeing Adam. You see, When you truly know Adam, you're aware that everything must meet the approval of Ada. She didn't like you. That's when I knew I needed to keep my eye on you. You must admit Dr. Vann, Adam pulled the wool over the eyes of some paramount people for twenty-one years with consummate duplicity," she laughed through a menacing smile.

She stepped behind the bench and picked up a solid oak table leg she had placed earlier. She stood behind him and with both hands she raised the heavy piece up over her head. She brought it down with a thundering blow. There was a resounding "crack" as it met his skull. He was lifeless within seconds as his body rolled off the bench and fell to the ground. The blood poured out onto her clean white flagstones. She shook her head as she dropped the table leg, picked up the tray and headed back to the house.

#

The telephone rang, and Ada picked up immediately, "Hello?"

"Hello, Ada darling, it's me. The last of our troubles is gone, now. Would you come next door right away and help me, please? Bring the shovel, dear – and don't forget the ammonia, and the mop and bucket."

" – Yes Mother, right away."

Adam hung up the telephone and rolled over to the mirror. He stood up and kicked the chair away as if he would never use it again. He slipped into a short, flowered summer dress and decided on pink lipstick that day. Then he reached over to a blonde wig on the dresser and slipped it on. He adjusted it and began brushing while staring at her reflection in the mirror. She smiled.

Time to rest, Adam. Have a good, long rest. I'll take it from here.

She sang, "Ba ba black sheep have you any wool..."

End

Afterword

Recently, I was asked by a close friend, "Where do your story ideas come from?" I'll talk about Splinter in a moment, but generally, the ideas that have gone into most of my work come from a combination of places. I often have dreams that are lucid, and colorful. I've heard it said that most people do not dream in color. I do, and I can almost always recall the details of those dreams; the colors; characters; places; events, etc.

My short story, The Peace of Pi, is an example of work that has come from a dream. Set in 19th Century England, this story played out in my mind like a movie. When I woke at around three o'clock in the morning, I hurried to my laptop. In less than an hour, I had a complete story – the quickest work I've done. By the way, what do I know about 19th Century England? Let me answer by saying, "Very little." Yet, the story was well received. One reader emailed me saying, "You wrote it as if you were there..."

Of course, some stories are inspired, or "triggered," as I put it, by life experiences. While some of those experiences are pleasant, as most of us have, I've experienced some unpleasant – even horrible – events in my life. I don't know for certain, but I think that incorporating some of those thoughts, dreams, and experiences – good, or bad – not only makes for good story telling, but serves as a coping mechanism, a way to let them go. Once penned, they no longer haunt me.

Splinter was a more complex piece than I like to write. Then why did I? I wanted to write something that would not just entertain, but require some thought by the reader. I enjoyed keeping a few pieces of the puzzle missing until that last paragraph. I hope I caught you off guard!

Additionally, some of the storyline events of Splinter are taken from my life (I'll keep you guessing), and some of it from my psychology background. Also, I wanted to honor my mother in some way (She passed away only a few months ago), so I used the setting of Milnor, ND, the tiny town where she grew up. She loved that little town and never lost her connection to her friends and family there – evidenced by the class reunions she attended. I don't know for certain if she would have liked the story, she was not always predicable, but I do know with all certainty that she would have felt honored by my using her hometown as the setting.

About the Author

Michael Bussa grew up in Schiller Park, IL, a small suburb of Chicago. He has an inordinate love of aviation; as a child he always knew he would work in the airline industry. He spent twenty-five years in the travel and hospitality industry, including a hotel, Amtrak, and four airlines.

"I was always fascinated with the idea that something so large could leave the ground so gracefully and stay in the air," he says. *"I mean, if I jumped off a cliff with my arms spread out like a bird, I'd plummet to my death!"*

Michael has found his niche writing short stories – he tells them in a twisted way that would make even Hitchcock proud!

Also By Michael Bussa

Fiction

The Peace Of Pi 2014

Ending In V 2014

Oh, Cedar, My Cedar 2016

FLOAT 2017

Specious (Coming 2017)

Non-Fiction

NOW BOARDING:

Confessions of a Stowaway 2010